Everybody Toots!

THIS IS AN UNCORRECTED PROOF COPY.
NOT FOR RESALE.
Publishing February 2024
Paperback ISBN: 978-1-78055-920-9

Publicity enquiries:
ALICE FURSE
Email:
ALICE.FURSE@MOMBOOKS.COM
Sales enquiries:
SALES@MOMBOOKS.COM

W www.mombooks.com/buster F Buster Books Y @BusterBooks @buster_books

Buster Books is an imprint of Michael O'Mara Books Limited,
9 Lion Yard, Tremadoc Road, London SW4 7NQ

Text copyright © Jonny Leighton 2024
Illustrations copyright © Mike Byrne 2024
Layout and design © Buster Books 2024

Printed and bound by CPI Group (UK) Ltd, Croydon, CR0 4YY

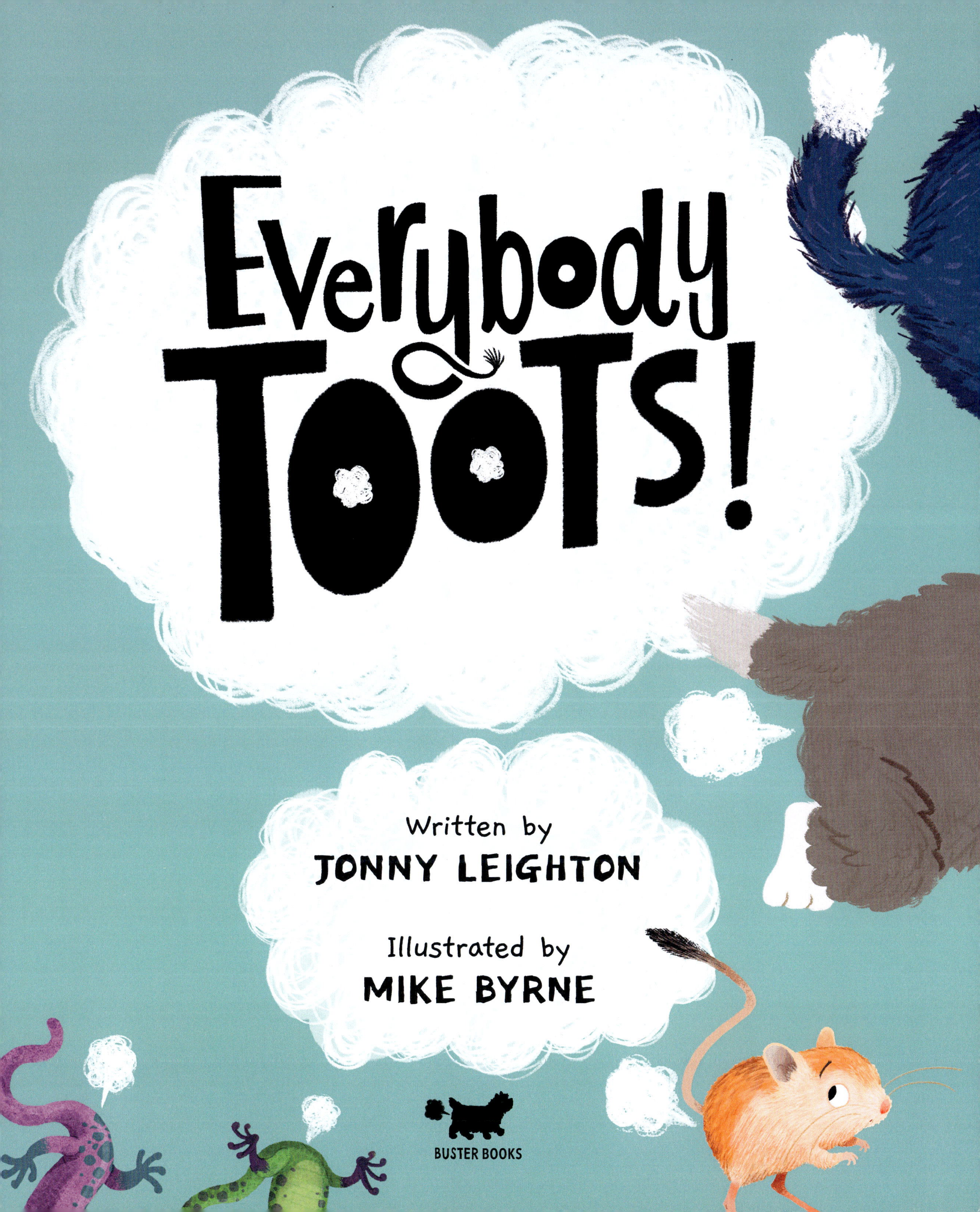

Everybody
TOOTS!

Written by
JONNY LEIGHTON

Illustrated by
MIKE BYRNE

BUSTER BOOKS

A squeaky, stinky toot slipped out of Jerboa's bottom.

"OOPS!" Jerboa said. "I meant to keep that in."

"KEEP IT IN?"

Elephant boomed. "Don't be silly.
You'd explode if you didn't let one out,
every now and again."

"EXPLODE?"

Jerboa said, alarmed.

"Yes. You'd take off like a rocket
and fly right out your boots.
Let me tell you something, friend,

EVERYBODY TOOTS!"

"There are creatures tooting high and low, you find them everywhere,

Like cats that toot on fluffy thrones, tails high in the air."

"Then there's mighty munching cows, chewing all day long.
They're PUMPY, TRUMPY, TOOT machines ..."

"You're right, and what a PONG!"

"A dog likes nothing better, than lifting up a leg,
with a **PUTT PUTT PUTT** from its butt butt butt..."

"And it smells like

ROTTEN
EGG!"

"Chimps
BREAK
WIND,

Sharks blow BUBBLES,

Worms' BIG WHOPPERS cause earthquake troubles."

"Mice are QUIET,

whales are LOUD,
and there's no worse toot than a seal's STINK CLOUD!"

"Lizards' toots go **POP!** and **SQUEAK!**

Snakes toot **GENTLY** in their sleep.

Penguin toots go **MEEP-MEEP-MEEP**, with a fishy stench that's quite unique.

And even though they're really small,
A spider's toot **OUT-STINKS** them all!"

"WOW," said Jerboa.
"There are tooters all over the place."

"INDEED," said Elephant.

"But I do wonder," said Jerboa. "Is it just animals that toot?"

Elephant sighed. "Oh no, Jerboa, you haven't understood at all ..."

"Little girls and little boys **TOOT** and blame it on their toys.

Adults **TOOT** and act as if they'd never even made a noise.

Grannies **TOOT** while on the go and couldn't be more proud.

Grandads **TOOT** quite openly and really love a crowd!"

"Monsters toot in perfect time, to their own tremendous tune,
Tooting while they're busy **DISCO-DANCING** round the room.

Robots grind their gears and let out
CLUNKY-CLANKY CLINKERS,

While superheroes save the world with
SUPER-POWER STINKERS."

"Dragons TOOT and dinos TOOT — every bottom sings,

Especially the ROYAL TRUMPETS, played by queens and kings!"

"I see," said Jerboa. "Everybody really does toot."

"Precisely," Elephant agreed.

"So," Jerboa said. "That must mean that you toot, too ..."

# "ME? TOOT?"

Elephant cried.

"HOW DARE YOU?

The only tooting I do is from my trunk.
I'd never let one slip ..."

... Unless there's no one looking
— then I just let

RIP!"